Charles M. Schulz

Calling All Cookies!

HarperHorizon
An Imprint of HarperCollins*Publishers*

First published in 1999 by HarperCollins*Publishers* Inc.
http://www.harpercollins.com
Copyright © 1999 United Feature Syndicate, Inc. All rights reserved.
HarperCollins ® and ♥ ® are trademarks of HarperCollins*Publishers* Inc. PEANUTS is a registered trademark of United Feature Syndicate, Inc.
PEANUTS © United Feature Syndicate, Inc. Based on the PEANUTS ® comic strip by Charles M. Schulz
http://www.snoopy.com
ISBN 0-694-01051-0
Printed in China

It's just that . . . somewhere . . . I'm not sure where, but . . . I can hear someone eating a chocolate chip cookie!

"I know what you want. You thought you heard a chocolate chip cookie calling you, didn't you?"

"Well, you didn't."

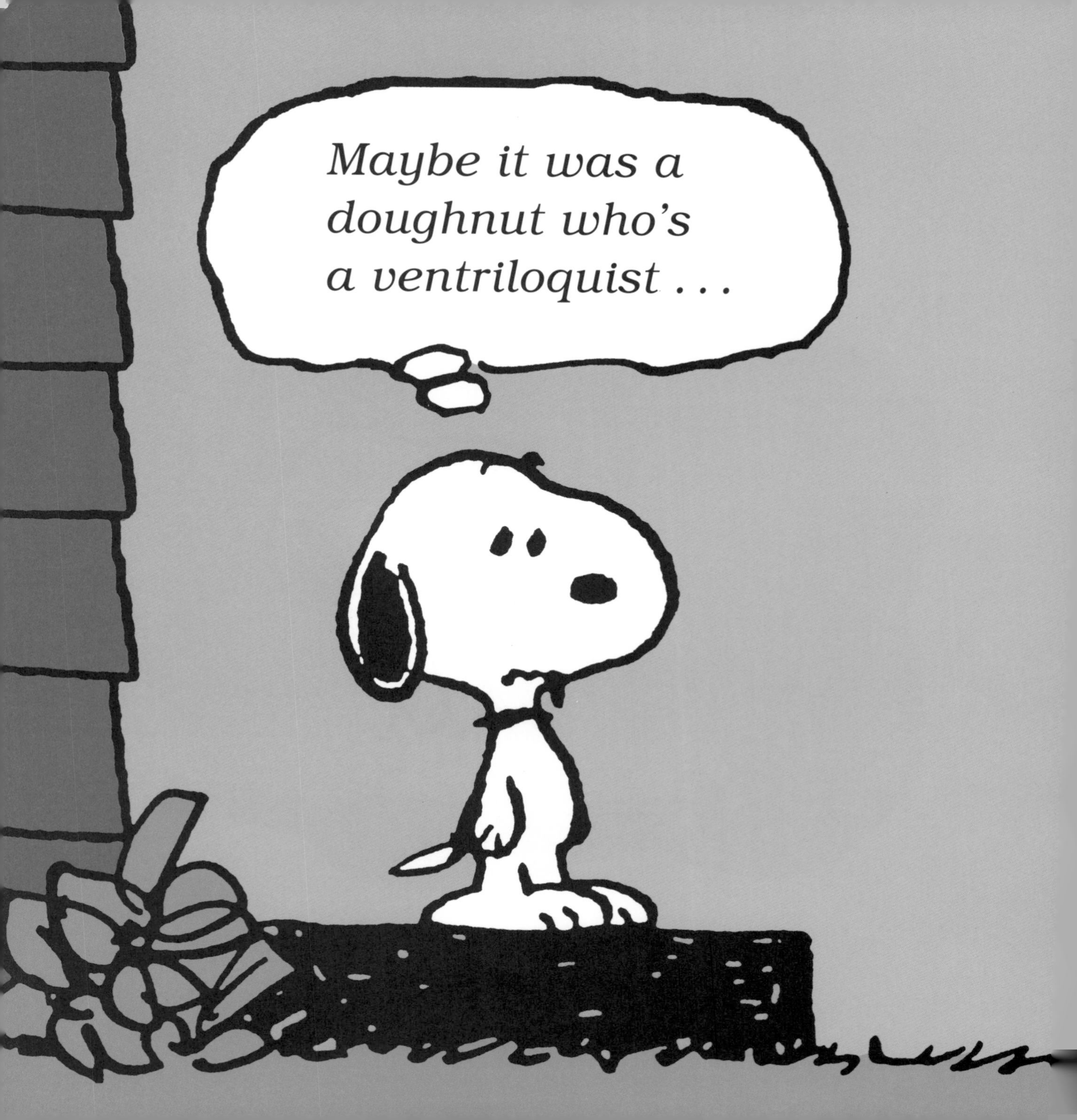
Maybe it was a doughnut who's a ventriloquist . . .

"Again? You must have good ears . . .
I never heard a thing . . ."

"Here you go. Four? How come you're taking four?"

"Hey! Empty?!"

"Ten chocolate chip cookies?! I was just about to fix your supper."

These are just warm-up cookies ... you should never eat without warming up first!

"You took all the cookies."

They were crying to get out of the jar . . .

"Just a minute . . . I'll go see . . ."

"No, the chocolate chip cookies weren't calling you ... in fact they were all sound asleep ... I didn't want to wake them because they've had kind of a hard day ..."

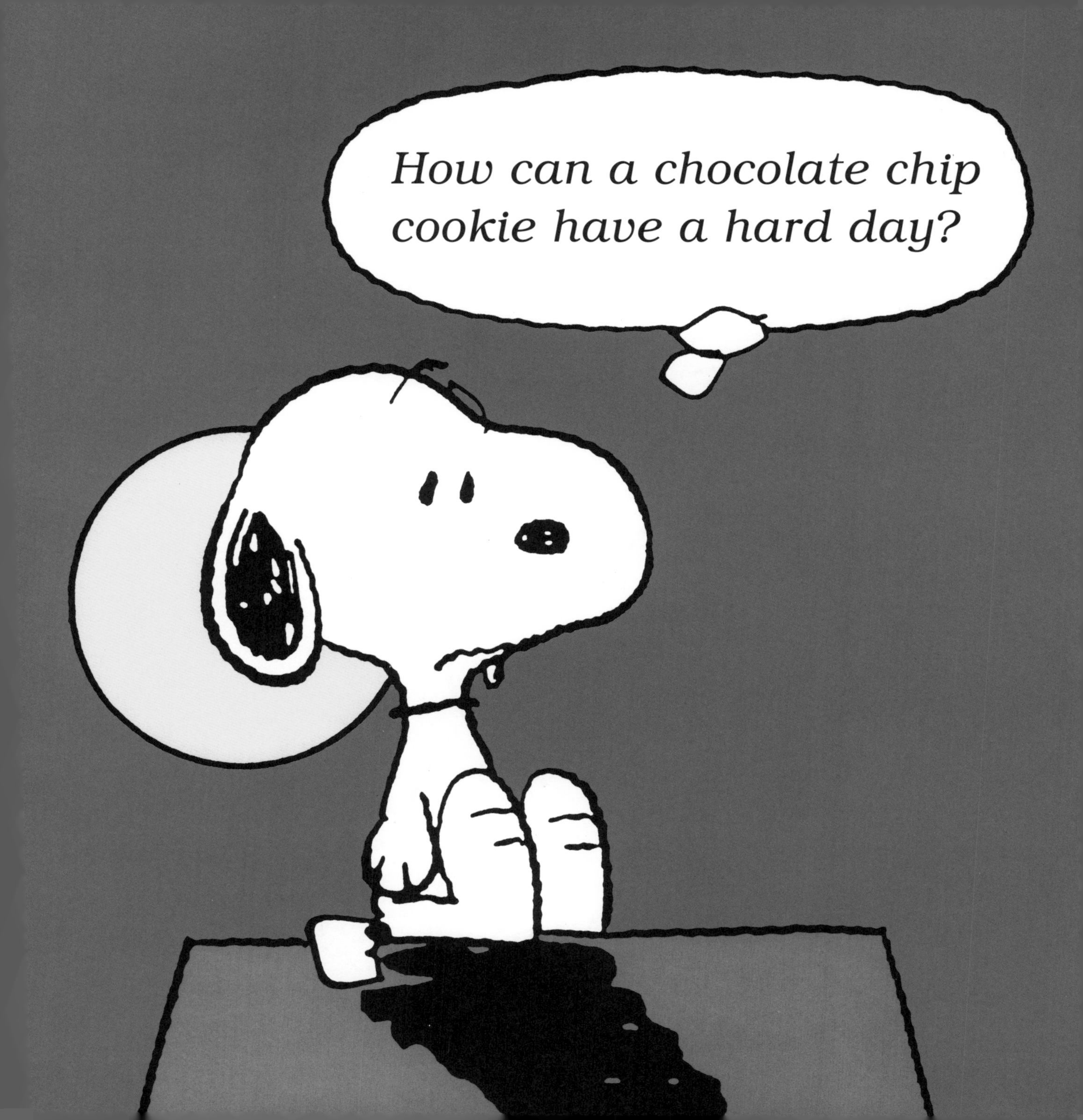
How can a chocolate chip cookie have a hard day?

"How did this cookie jar get empty again?"